NOTE TO PARENTS

Based on the beloved Walt Disney motion picture *Bambi,* this book focuses on what happens when Bambi explores his forest home with his friends Thumper and Flower. Young and inexperienced at first, the friends learn, play, and grow together as they witness nature's changes through the year.

During his first winter, Bambi learns to miss his friends. In the springtime, the friends are happy to be together again. But they are more grown-up now, and they are making special new friends. Bambi worries that Thumper and Flower won't like him anymore. But his own special friend, Faline, tells him what he's really known all along: There is room for all kinds of different friends in everyone's life. Making new friends doesn't have to mean losing the old ones.

This book recounts one memorable episode from the movie that will help children learn an important lesson about the value of friendship.

WALT DISNEY'S
Bambi
and His Forest Adventures
A BOOK ABOUT FRIENDSHIP

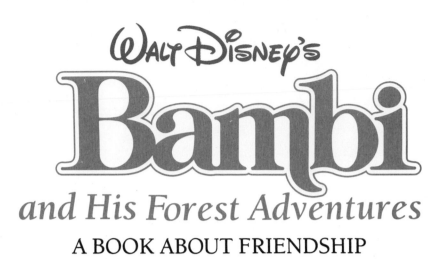

A GOLDEN BOOK • NEW YORK
Western Publishing Company, Inc., Racine, Wisconsin 53404

Bambi the fawn and Thumper the rabbit were friends.
They played together every day.

Every morning Thumper hopped along the forest path to
the thicket where Bambi lived. He thumped his hind foot on
a hollow log, and he called, "Hey, Bambi! Come on out!"

Bambi came out, and he and Thumper set off to explore
the woods.

Thumper was a little older than Bambi, so Bambi
thought the rabbit must be very wise. Bambi listened
carefully to everything Thumper said.

One day a bird flew to a branch above Bambi's head. It perched there and sang a few notes. Then it spread its wings and flew away.

Thumper wanted to share the things he knew with his friend. "That's a bird," said Thumper.

"Bird!" cried Bambi.

A butterfly fluttered down and settled on Bambi's tail.

Bambi stared. The butterfly flew like a bird, but it was different.

"Bird?" said Bambi.

Thumper laughed. "That's not a bird. That's a butterfly."

They came to a clearing where the forest floor was covered with blossoms. Bambi stood very still. He waited for the flowers to flutter or fly. They didn't stir.

"Butterflies?" said Bambi.

"No, no!" cried Thumper. "Those aren't butterflies. They're flowers."

"Flowers!" said Bambi. He bent to sniff a daisy. Suddenly he was looking straight into the eyes of another animal.

"Flower?" said Bambi.

Thumper laughed. "That's no flower!" he cried. "That's a skunk."

The little skunk smiled shyly. "He can call me Flower, if
he wants to," said the skunk.

Bambi and Thumper did call the little skunk Flower.
From that day on they had another friend.

All through the summer Bambi, Thumper, and Flower
played together. Each shared what he learned with the
others.

When Bambi looked into a quiet pond and saw a young deer looking back, he told his friends about it. They hurried to look.

Thumper saw a lively young rabbit.

Flower saw a baby skunk with a white stripe.

When it was very warm, Flower showed Bambi and
Thumper how to play hide-and-seek in the cool shadows.
Flower knew the best places to hide—the hollow under
Friend Owl's tree, for instance. If Friend Owl looked down
and saw Flower there, he never gave away the hiding place.

On cooler days Bambi and Thumper raced the wind across the meadow while Flower watched.

Bambi won the race one day, and Flower cheered for him. Then Flower cheered for Thumper.

Bambi was puzzled. "Why are you cheering for Thumper when I won the race?"

"I'm cheering for you both because you're both my friends," Flower said, "no matter whether you win or lose."

One morning Bambi felt a chill in the air. He looked out of his thicket, and he saw that everything had changed. Leaves were falling from the trees to the forest floor.

Thumper hurried along the path. He thumped on the hollow log. "Bambi, come and see!" he called. "Something is happening to our woods!"

Friend Owl looked down from the big oak tree. "Whooo's making all that noise?" he hooted.

"It's me, Friend Owl," said Thumper. "Do you know what's happening to our trees? They're all different colours! And the leaves are falling off!"

"That means winter is coming," said Friend Owl. "Soon it will snow."

"Snow?" said Bambi. "What's snow?"

"It's white stuff," said Friend Owl. "It falls from the sky and covers the ground."

"White stuff that falls from the sky?" echoed Bambi.

"You made that up!" said Thumper.

"You'll see!" said Friend Owl.

Bambi woke one morning to see that the ground was all white.

Thumper came sliding down a snowdrift. "Bambi, come on!" he cried. "It's snow, just like Friend Owl said. And it's fun!"

The snowdrifts *were* fun, and the water in the pond was frozen. Thumper could skate on it!

Bambi tried to skate, but his hard little hooves weren't right for skating. His front legs went one way, and his back legs went the other. He fell, and he couldn't get up again until Thumper helped him.

"Let's go and get Flower!" said Thumper.
Flower was at home, but he wouldn't come out to play.
"Flowers sleep through the winter," he told his friends.

The days grew colder. Thumper often stayed in his burrow now, huddled close to his mother to keep warm.

Bambi felt lonely. "How long will winter last?" he asked his mother. "I want it to get warm again, so I can play in the meadow with Thumper and Flower."

"Be patient," said Bambi's mother. "Winter will pass."

Winter did pass. One morning Thumper came thumping on the hollow log near Bambi's thicket.

"Come out, Bambi!" cried Thumper. "The snow's gone from the meadow. We can play race-the-wind again!"

Bambi came out. He saw green grass everywhere and felt the warm breeze.

Flower appeared, rubbing the sleep from his eyes. The three friends were together again!

The next day Bambi went to see if Thumper wanted to play. But when he came to Thumper's burrow, Bambi saw his friend playing with another rabbit—and she wasn't one of Thumper's sisters.

"Thumper has a new friend," Bambi thought sadly. "I guess he doesn't want to play with me anymore."

So, all alone, Bambi went to find Flower. But near Flower's den he saw his friend playing with a pretty little skunk.

"Flower has a new friend, too," Bambi thought. "I guess no one wants to play with me."

Bambi felt just as lonely as he had during the winter. He walked along by himself till he came to the pond. Then he gazed into the water at his own sad face. Suddenly he saw another face in the water—the face of a beautiful young doe.

"Hello," she said. "My name is Faline. I'd like to be your friend."

"Oh, would you?" said Bambi. "My old friends don't like me anymore. They have new friends."

"That doesn't mean they don't like *you*," said Faline. "I'm sure they're still your friends."

Bambi liked his new friend, and he found out that Faline was right about his old friends. Soon Thumper and Flower came to introduce their new friends to Bambi.

Bambi said, "I thought you didn't like me anymore. But Faline told me you can have all kinds of friends—old and new, big and small, boys and girls. It doesn't matter."

"Right!" said Thumper. "Come on! Let's play!"

And all the old and new friends played tag under the shady trees of their forest home.